The Last Day of Kindergarten

by **Nancy Loewen**   illustrated by **Sachiko Yoshikawa**

Marshall Cavendish Children

Marshall Cavendish Corporation
99 White Plains Road
Tarrytown, NY 10591
www.marshallcavendish.us/kids

Library of Congress Cataloging-in-Publication Data
Loewen, Nancy
The last day of kindergarten / by Nancy Loewen ; illustrated by Sachiko
Yoshikawa. — 1st ed.
p. cm.
Summary: As she prepares for her graduation ceremony, a first grader-to-be
remembers her enjoyable year in kindergarten.
ISBN 978-0-7614-5807-4
[1. Kindergarten—Fiction. 2. Schools—Fiction.] I. Yoshikawa, Sachiko,
ill. II. Title.
PZ7.L8268Las 2011   [E]—dc22   2010001225

The illustrations were rendered digitally in mixed media.
Editor: Robin Benjamin
Printed in China (E)
First edition
10 9 8 7 6 5 4 3 2 1

Marshall Cavendish
Children

For my daughter, Helena, whose tearful and triumphant
last day of kindergarten inspired this story
—N.L.

To Kinu and all her friends in the Sunshine Garden
Special thanks to Mikako Miyazaki
—S.Y.

Today is the last day of kindergarten.

I wish it were the FIRST. Then I'd meet
Mrs. Popinski all over again.

I'd hang my very own backpack on my very own hook.

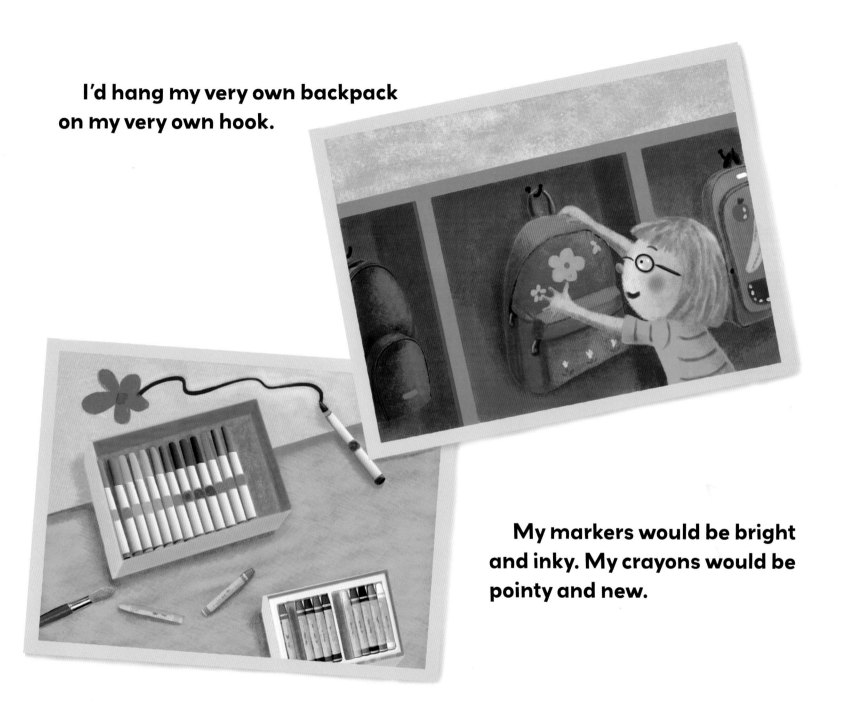

My markers would be bright and inky. My crayons would be pointy and new.

If it were the FIRST day of kindergarten, I'd have so much to look forward to this year.

I'd play House or Grocery Store during Creative Playtime.

I'd dress up as a tiger for the Halloween parade.

I'd lose my first tooth biting into
Sammy McGregor's birthday cupcakes.

But today is the LAST day of kindergarten.
We don't read stories. We don't work on our
numbers or letters. Instead, we wash the tables.

We throw out the stubbiest crayons and the dried-up paints.

We take our pictures off the walls.

Mrs. Popinski gathers us into a circle for Sharing Time. It's the last time we'll ever sit criss-cross applesauce together.

"I am so proud of all of you," Mrs. Popinski says. "You've learned so much this year! But kindergarten is ending. Summer is beginning. What are your favorite things about summer?"

Staying up late

Swimming

Picnics in the park

Running through the sprinkler

Eating blue raspberry ice pops on the front steps

"Let's talk about first grade," Mrs. Popinski says. "What are you looking forward to the most?"

Eating lunch in the cafeteria

Field trips

Writing stories

Recess

Playing on the
big kids' playground

Making new friends

"Wow," Mrs. Popinski says. "You're going
to be fantastic first graders. I can just tell."
She looks at the clock and stands up.
"Okay, class. It's time!"

We put on the funny flat hats that we made out of poster board and yarn.
We make sure our faces are clean.
   Then we line up and walk down the hall to the auditorium.

I peek over Mason's shoulder and see a
crowd—people pointing cameras at the stage,
little brothers and sisters squirming on laps.

Oh! I see Mommy and Daddy! And Grandma and Grandpa and Aunt Dee. This afternoon they're going to take me out for ice cream, and I can order whatever I want.

Mr. Meyer starts playing a serious song on the piano. It makes me want to cry. It makes me want to march.

It makes me want to stand up straight and tall.

This is it.

I'm walking onto the stage.

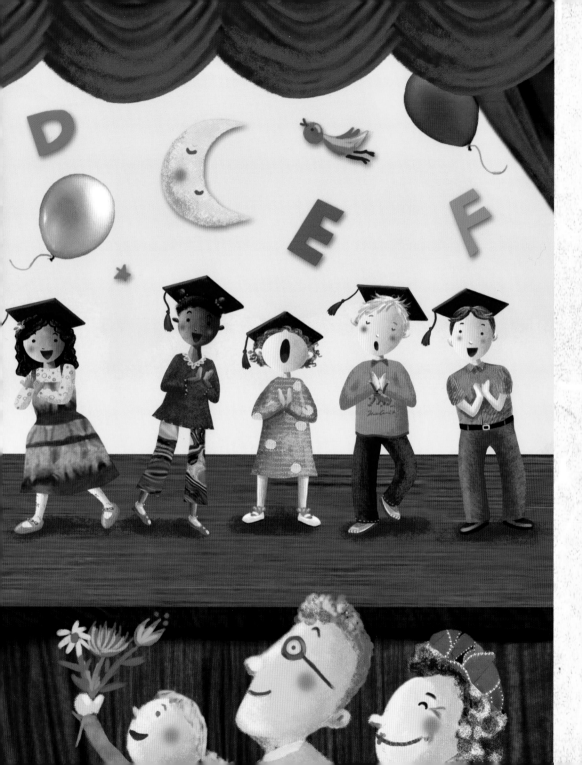

I'm reciting our ABC farewell poem without making any mistakes. I'm singing "Zip-A-Dee-Doo-Dah" and clapping in all the right places.

I'm shaking hands with the principal.

Kindergarten

is

over....

I did it!

First grade, here I come!

2/11